Complete your Angelina Ballerina DVD Collection!

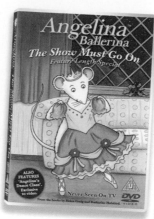

For further information, please visit
www.angelinaballerina.com

This Angelina Ballerina Annual belongs to

....

Angelina Ballerina™

Annual 2007

Contents

EGMONT

We bring stories to life

First published in Great Britain 2006 by Egmont UK Limited
239 Kensington High Street, London W8 6SA

Angelina Ballerina © 2006 Helen Craig Ltd. and Katharine Holabird.
The Angelina Ballerina name and character and the dancing Angelina logo
are trademarks of HIT Entertainment Limited, Katharine Holabird and Helen Craig.
Reg. U.S. Pat. & Tm. Off.

Stories adapted from original scripts by Laura Beaumont,
Paul Larson and Jan Page.

Meet Angelina Ballerina™

I may be just a little white mouseling now, but I have a BIG, BIG dream. I'm going to work very hard so that one day I'll be a famous ballerina!

Angelina and the Mouseling family

Angelina Mouseling lives in Mouseland, in a village called Chipping Cheddar. She lives with her family in an old cottage with a roof made of thatch.

Angelina is a wonderful dancer, and her dream is to be a great ballerina one day and dance in the world's most famous theatres.

Angelina always **tries** to be good – but she doesn't always manage it! She enjoys fun and adventures far too much to be good **all** the time!

"oh, I so want to be a famous ballerina one day!"

Polly is Angelina's baby sister. She's tiny and cute, and although Angelina was a bit jealous when she first arrived, she can't imagine life without her now!

"Having a little sister is the BEST fun!"

Mr Maurice Mouseling is Angelina's dad. He works hard running the local newspaper, the Mouseland Gazette, but he's never too busy to play his fiddle for Angelina to dance to.

"I love it when Dad comes home with a new joke to tell me!"

Mrs Matilda Mouseling is Angelina's mum. She's a great cook and Angelina will tell you that she makes the most lovely ballet costumes. She's kind and patient, even when Angelina is being a bit difficult.

"You should taste Mum's Cheddar cheese pies. They're the best in the whole wide world!"

Grandma is very kind. She sometimes tells Angelina to watch her manners, but that's because she wants her to grow up to be a real lady.

"Grandma is a sweetie!"

Grandpa may be old and has to walk with a stick, but he's still full of fun.

"I love Grandpa's stories – especially the scary ones!"

Angelina's very special friends

Alice Nimbletoes is Angelina's best friend in the whole wide world. She's happy and cheerful and always has a smile on her face – even when Angelina is being silly or stubborn!

"Alice Nimbletoes – my best friend!"

Alice thinks life is fun, and she just loves to laugh. The silliest things make her giggle – and when Alice starts to giggle it's not long before everyone else is laughing, too!

Alice often has her head stuck in some book or other, so she knows lots and lots of things about all sorts of stuff.

Like Angelina, Alice loves to dance. She's not as good as Angelina, but she's a hard worker and she always tries hard. She can be a bit clumsy sometimes, and often trips up over her own paws!

Miss Lilly is Angelina's ballet teacher – and her very special all-time hero.

Miss Lilly comes from faraway Dacovia and she has great style. She wears really colourful dresses with long, flowing scarves – and lots and lots of bright jewellery.

Miss Lilly used to be a great ballerina herself. She doesn't perform on the stage now, but she is determined that the pupils at her ballet school will be wonderful dancers, just as she was. Her favourite pupil is Angelina and she calls her, "my darlink!"

Miss Lilly just lives for dance, and the shows she puts on at her ballet school are the highlight of the Chipping Cheddar year. They're full of light, colour, movement, grace and drama – just like Miss Lilly!

"Miss Lilly – the best ballet teacher a mouseling ever had!"

Angelina's friends

Henry is Angelina's young cousin. He just adores Angelina and follows her around all the time because he always wants to do just what she wants to do.

"Henry can be a bit annoying sometimes, but I love him really!"

William Longtail is one of Angelina's very best friends. He's quiet and a bit shy and – this is a secret, so don't say a word! – he just LOVES Angelina.

"William sometimes gets a bit tongue-tied and flustered when I'm around. I wonder why?"

Sammy is a cheeky, naughty mouse – which is just how Angelina likes her friends to be! He's always coming up with new pranks and tricks to play on Angelina.

"Sammy prefers sport to ballet, but I still like him!"

...and enemies

Penelope and Priscilla Pinkpaws are in the same class as Angelina at Miss Lilly's ballet school. Angelina likes all the other pupils – except them! The twins are spoiled and always have the best of everything: best toys, best clothes, best ballet costumes.

The twins always like to get their own way and they can be very sneaky, so they're not very popular, especially with Angelina and her friends.

"I call Penelope and Priscilla Pinkpaws the terrible twins – because they are!"

The ballet tickets

1

It was early morning and Angelina was in a hurry. She took a bite of pancake then looked around. "Where's my coat?" she asked.

2

Her friend Alice held it up. "It's here," she said, as Angelina grabbed it – and put her arm into the wrong sleeve. "Oh, NO!" said Angelina.

3

"What's the hurry?" asked Mr Mouseling. Mrs Mouseling explained. "The tickets go on sale for Mimi and Mikel Whiskersev this morning."

4

"The MOST wonderful dancers in the ENTIRE universe!" said Angelina. "Come on, Alice, if we miss the bus it's an hour till the next one. BYE!"

Angelina and Alice were too late! The bus went without them and it was a whole hour before they got to the Theatre Royal. "At last!" said Angelina.

The box office manager gave tickets to the Pinkpaws twins – then closed the window! "Sorry," he said. "Those were the last tickets. We're sold out."

Angelina could not believe it. "Those tickets should be ours," she said to Alice on the way home. "We have to find a way to get them! We HAVE to!"

At school the next morning, Angelina asked if the Pinkpaws twins would swap their tickets for a bead necklace. "You **are** joking!" said Penelope.

But Priscilla couldn't take her eyes off Angelina's ballerina music box. "No, don't give her that!" said Alice. "It was your birthday present!"

"Yes, it's too good to swap," said Angelina. "So we'll DANCE for it. Whoever does the most pirouettes gets the music box AND the ballet tickets!"

Angelina and the twins were soon spinning and turning. "Keep going, Priscilla!" cried Penelope. "You can beat them, Angelina!" said William.

Suddenly, Angelina's necklace broke and she slipped on the beads and fell over! Priscilla grabbed the music box. "Mine, I think!" she said.

13

After school, Angelina and Alice went back to the theatre. They were going to pretend to be Miss Lilly so they could ask the Whiskersevs for tickets!

14

But the plan failed when Alice trod on the long cloak they were wearing. It fell to the ground, and the manager sent them back outside again.

15

Angelina didn't give up. She stood on Alice's shoulders to jump in through a window, but landed at the manager's feet. "Oops," said Angelina.

16

That evening, Angelina was so upset that she couldn't eat any of Mrs Mouseling's famous cheese pie, her very favourite supper.

"What's this sad face for?" asked Mr Mouseling. "The ballet's tonight, and I'm not going!" said Angelina. "There are no tickets left."

Mr Mouseling put some tickets on the table! "Are you sure?" he asked. "I've got three!" Angelina could not believe her eyes. She was delighted!

That evening, Angelina and Alice watched as Mimi and Mikel danced the final scene of the ballet. "Encore!" they cried. "More! Bravo!"

They had the very best seats – but Penelope and Priscilla were sitting right at the back of the theatre. They could hardly see the stage!

Later, Mr Mouseling took Angelina and Alice to a door with a big gold star on it. "You have a little job to do for me before we go home," he said.

The door opened and inside were Mimi and Mikel! "Angelina is going to interview you for the Mouseland Gazette!" Miss Lilly told them.

A few days later, Angelina sat with her dad as they looked at the Mouseland Gazette together. "Well done," said Mr Mouseling. "It's a good interview."

Angelina smiled. "Thanks, Dad," she said. "Of course, I'm going to be a great ballerina when I grow up. But maybe I'll be a great reporter as well!"

It was SO cold at the start of the year that I thought I would freeze! It's a good job I had the warm hat and scarf Grandma knitted for me!

I don't like the cold much, but I LOVE the snow! When I woke up one Saturday morning and looked outside, the whole village was covered in a soft white snowy blanket.

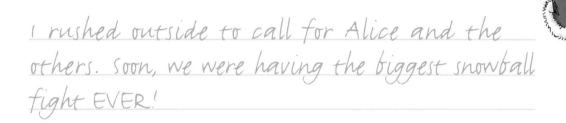

I rushed outside to call for Alice and the others. Soon, we were having the biggest snowball fight EVER!

Angelina's dad took some photos of the snowball fight. These are two of them. Circlc 5 things that are different in picture 2.

2

February was really cold, but there was no snow to play in so we were stuck indoors. It was soooo dull and I was sooooo bored until one day Mum helped me make some cheese cookies and cherry buns. They were yummy!

Colour in the number of cheese cookies to match the number in the box.

2

4

Now draw a cherry for each bun to match the number in the box, then colour them in.

3

5

In March the sun started to shine at last! I ran outside to play in the garden — until Mum called me back inside. "It's time for some spring cleaning," she said. Can you guess

whose room we tidied first? Yes, my messy bedroom!

Is **your** bedroom as messy and untidy as Angelina's?

What do you do in March? Write about it, then draw a spring picture.

One day as the bell rang for the end of school, Miss Chalk spoke to the mouselings. "Don't forget that tomorrow is Show and Tell Day," she told them. "You must all bring in something to tell the class about."

"I'm going to make a giant chocolate cake for my Show and Tell," said Alice. "Then we can eat it for lunch! What are you going to bring, Angelina?"

"Wait and see!" said Angelina.

Next morning, Angelina set off from home for Show and Tell Day with – her baby sister, Polly! She and Sammy were in

such a rush that they bumped into each other and Sammy's yellow yo-yo flew into the air, bounced off his nose – and disappeared!

"Hey, my yo-yo! Where is it?" said Sammy, looking to see if it had fallen down the drain.

"Lellow o-yo!" said Polly. "Lellow o-yo!"

"Where is it then, smartypants?" Sammy asked Polly.

"Hey, don't call my sister Smartypants!" said Angelina. "She ..."

Suddenly, Miss Chalk appeared. "Sammy, Angelina. Go into class, this instant!"

Angelina bent down to pick up Polly – but she was gone! "Polly? POLLY!" said Angelina, going into the classroom to look for her.

The others were waiting to Show and Tell. Priscilla had

her ballerina music box, William had a wooden plane, and Flora had her pet grasshopper in a little wooden cage.

Angelina looked under the desks. "Did she come in here?" she asked Alice.

"Who?"

"Polly, of course!" said Angelina.

"Polly?" said Alice. "You brought POLLY for Show and Tell Day?"

Just then, Miss Chalk told Angelina to sit down.

"But Miss, it's P ..." said Angelina.

"SIT DOWN!" ordered Miss Chalk, and Angelina decided she'd better do as she was told.

Outside the classroom, Polly crawled into the school storeroom.

"O-yo! Lellow o-yo!" she said. She grabbed a jug and blue paint went everywhere! Then she crawled out, saying, "Lellow o-yo!"

In the classroom, Miss Chalk chose Flora to show and tell. Flora was about to tell the others about her grasshopper – but Angelina had let it out of its cage to cause a distraction while she looked for Polly!

While the others were busy looking for the grasshopper, Angelina pulled Alice outside to search for Polly. Sammy was right behind them.

"Where **is** she?" cried Angelina.

"Did you see where it went?" asked Sammy.

"Polly is not an IT!" said Angelina angrily.

"I don't mean Polly, I mean my yo-yo!" said Sammy, going out into the playground to look for his yo-yo.

Angelina and Alice went into the storeroom to look for Polly. There was paint and water everywhere – but there was no sign of Polly.

Next they found a pile of books that had been pulled off the bookshelves – but there was still no sign of Polly.

Polly was in the playground. She crawled to the yellow Big Cheese playhouse, looked inside – and saw Sammy's yo-yo!

"Lellow o-yo!" said Polly, wriggling in through one of the windows. She got the yo-yo, but she couldn't get out again. She was stuck!

Sammy was still looking for his yo-yo when he heard Miss Chalk calling his name, so he hid in the Big Cheese – and found Polly! He smiled when he saw what she was holding in her paw.

"My yo-yo!" said Sammy, taking it from her. "You've found it, Polly!"

Polly didn't like that at all! "WAAAAAAAA!" she cried.

"Shh!" said Sammy. "Shh! Be quiet!"

But Polly just cried harder than ever. She made so much noise that Miss Chalk, Angelina and Alice rushed to the Big Cheese to see what was going on.

Miss Chalk peered in through the window. "A baby?" she said. "Sammy Watts, you've got some explaining to do!"

Miss Chalk led them back into school as Sammy tried to explain. "So I went to look for her, and I heard this crying, and there she was in the Big Cheese, stuck!"

"Please ask your mother to see me later," Miss Chalk told Sammy. He thought he was in BIG trouble until she added, "I want to tell her how you rescued Polly. You're a hero!"

Then Miss Chalk turned to Angelina. "As for you, Angelina, you really should take better care of your sister. You owe Sammy a thank you. A **BIG** thank you."

As Miss Chalk walked away Angelina said, "You're not going to get away with this, Sammy! I'm going to tell Miss Chalk what really happened!"

"No, please don't, Angelina," said Sammy. "Please! I'll give you anything, ANYTHING!"

Angelina smiled. "Really? Anything?" she asked.

A few minutes later, Angelina stood in front of the class showing and telling about Polly. "Looking after a baby is hard work," she said, pointing to Sammy, who was sitting with Polly on his knee.

"It's not easy keeping a baby happy. So I want you to say an extra big thank you to Sammy here for giving Polly his very best yellow yo-yo to play with."

Angelina paused then spoke again. "And please remember never to let whoever you're looking after out of your sight," she said. "Even if it's a grasshopper!"

April is one of my
favourite months
of the year because
it's when spring is
really here.

The trees are
covered in pink
and white blossom,
the birds sing,
and everything is
green and new!

Look carefully. Which of the spring things here can you
find in the big picture? Draw a ✓ for yes, or a ✗ for no.

1 2 3 4 5 6

Answer:
Little pictures 2, 3, 5 and 6 are part of the big picture.

Angelina the mouse detective

1

2

One spring morning, Alice and Henry were playing catch in the lane outside Angelina's house. "Your turn, Alice!" said Henry.

Henry threw the ball, but it was too high for Alice and it flew into Mrs Hodgepodge's garden, bounced, and hit the door of her shed.

3

4

"Sorry," said Henry. "Can we have our ball back, please?" Mrs Hodgepodge shook her head and put the ball with a pile of others. "NO!" she said.

When Henry and Alice met Angelina outside her house, she was reading the new Monty the Mouse Detective book, *The Case of the Missing Cheese*.

When they got to Miss Lilly's house, she was talking to Inspector Scrabbler about a missing gnome. "He had a red cap and a broken arm," she said.

"We'll soon find the thief who stole your garden gnome," said the Inspector. "We need Monty the Mouse Detective!" said Henry.

"Monty the Mouse Detective might not be here," said Angelina. "But ANGELINA the Mouse Detective IS! Come on!"

Later, when Miss Lilly went out, Angelina, Alice and Henry went into her garden and Angelina read from her book. "First we dust for pawprints," she said.

9

10

"There might be some on the gate," said Alice. But Henry was doing his gymnastics on the gate and it was covered in HIS pawprints.

Angelina read her book again. "Monty would look for clues," she said, as Henry handed her a gardening glove he had found. "You're a genius!" she said.

11

12

Just then a paw appeared and took the glove. "My gardenink glove," said Miss Lilly. "I haf been looking everywhere for it! Thank you, darlinks!"

"Monty would find suspects," said Angelina, as Captain Millar popped out from behind a bush with a sack, then rushed off across the road.

"Nasty little red-capped things," he muttered. "Spoil everyone's gardens, they do." Angelina and the others gasped. "He's our suspect!" said Angelina.

They were following Captain Millar when he met Mrs Pinkpaws. SHE had a bag, as well! "I've only found a few," she said. "Not everyone has them."

"Well, let's take them to the bonfire," said Captain Millar. "They're going to Miss Chalk's house!" said Alice. "They're all in on it!" said Angelina.

"What would Monty do?" asked Alice. Angelina read her book. "He would confront them!" she said. "And that's what I'm going to do!"

"So you thought you could get away with it, eh?" said Angelina, tipping out the sack of ... red-capped toadstools. "Oops, sorry," said Angelina.

Alice took Henry home, leaving Angelina to walk home on her own ... but she stopped when she saw a shape in Mrs Hodgepodge's shed window.

"What would Monty do?" said Angelina bravely. "He would go to the door, turn the handle and – catch the gnome thief red-handed!"

But when Angelina saw a shadow, she screamed. "Arrrrgh!" she cried, and the shadow screamed even louder: "ARRRRGH!"

21

"Angelina?" said a voice from the shed. "Mrs Hodgepodge?" said Angelina. She stepped into the shed, which was full of garden gnomes!

22

"You're the gnome thief!" said Angelina. "No, I didn't steal them," said Mrs Hodgepodge. "They were uncared for. I was painting and mending them."

23

Next morning, Miss Lilly's gnome was back in her garden. He had new paint and his broken arm was mended. "I wonder how that happened?" said Alice.

24

Later on, Henry bounced his ball into Mrs Hodgepodge's garden and it bounced back! "People aren't always what they seem ..." said Angelina.

In May, we all wore flowers in our fur and danced around a Maypole holding long ribbons. Oh, it was such fun, and lots of people came to watch. Dad put our picture on the front page of the Mouseland Gazette!

Can you see Angelina and Alice in the picture – and baby Polly? What do you do in May? Write about it, then draw a picture.

May was such a lovely month that one day on the way home from school I felt so happy I just jumped for joy – but I didn't look where I was jumping!

Look at the pictures of Angelina and her next door neighbour, Mrs Hodgepodge. Can you tell the story in your own words?

1

2

Angelina's princess dance

After ballet class one day, Miss Lilly had some news. "Next veek you vill be dancing at ... the Royal Palace!" she told the mouselings. "And you, Angelina, will direct the show."

Later, Angelina wondered which ballet to put on. "It's in a real castle, so the show has to be really **princessy**!" she said.

"Like Sleeping Beauty?" said Alice.

"Perfect!" said Angelina.

"We'll all have jobs to do, as well as parts to play," she told the mouselings. "William, you will be Prince Charming and help with the sets. Alice, you will be Carnation Fairy and be in charge of costumes. Felicity and Flora will be Lily Fairy and Daisy Fairy and be in charge of make-up."

"Oooo, good!" said Flora.

"Henry is the Page Boy," said Angelina. "And I will be Princess Aurora and Director!"

"What are **we**?" asked Priscilla Pinkpaws.

"You're Wicked Fairy and Ugly Page," replied Angelina. "Perfect parts for you. Sammy will do special effects."

The mouselings **loved** the Royal Palace!

The King showed Henry a painting of Lord Stilton of Cheeseborough. "He's a ghost who goes around wailing '*More cheeeeeese!*'" he told him.

Rehearsals had started when Queen Seraphina asked Angelina if her daughters, Princess Sophie and Princess Valentine, could dance in the ballet.

How could Angelina refuse? "Of course," she said. "Princess Sophie will be Carnation Fairy and Princess Valentine will be ... Princess Aurora."

But the princesses were not good dancers. Not only that, they complained about everything: the steps were too hard, their shoes were slippery – and they wanted much sparklier costumes. Then they told Angelina the ballet had to have TWO princesses in it!

"And they stopped rehearsals so Flora and Felicity could bring them sandwiches to eat!" Angelina told Alice. "Oh, what have I done?"

Henry and the youngest princess, Phoebe, had fun pretending to be Lord Stilton's ghost!

When William heard them wailing, "*More cheeeeese!*" he ran off in a panic.

When Henry and Phoebe wailed at Sammy, who was working on his special effects in

one of the dungeons, he ran out, locking them in. They found a secret doorway, and soon found themselves in a maze of dark tunnels ...

Angelina was angry with the princesses. "They're horrible!" she told Alice. "They said the stage beds were too hard, so I used their own beds, and now they say there's no room for them to dance!"

Angelina had had enough. She decided to get tough. "No more Miss Nice Mouse!" she said at the next rehearsal. "It's time for work, HARD work!"

Sammy tried out his special effect, but the explosion covered the stage and costumes in smoke and soot. Then the set fell down ...

Angelina exploded, too. She shouted at the mouselings and said everything was their fault! Everything!

Now Alice and the others had had enough and they stormed off the stage.

"You can do the show with your precious princesses!" said Alice.

Later on, Angelina was walking along a corridor when she overheard Valentine and Sophie talking in their bedroom.

"We've been so – *sniff!* – mean," said Sophie.

"Yes, poor – *sniff!* – Angelina," added Valentine.

When they saw Angelina, the princesses tried to explain.

"Mum wanted us to be in the ballet, but we know we're not good enough," said Valentine.

"We thought if we kept complaining, you'd get rid of us," added Sophie.

Later, Flora had news for the mouselings. "There's a meeting on stage!" she told the others. "Angelina has something to say!"

When Angelina told them how sorry she was they all agreed that the show must go on.

That evening, the audience took their seats in the Palace Theatre and when the music began, **three** Sleeping Beauty princesses danced across the

stage – Valentine, Sophie ... and Angelina!

Under the theatre, the secret passage led Henry and Phoebe to a trapdoor where Priscilla and Penelope were waiting to make their entrance. Sammy pulled a lever and there was a flash and a bang. All four of them flew up on to the stage. "Dance!" said Henry.

The ballet ended when William kissed one, two, three Sleeping Beauties. They awoke as the audience cheered and clapped.

Queen Seraphina gave Angelina a huge bouquet of flowers then put her crown on Angelina's head!

"Now you look like a real princess!" whispered Alice.

At the banquet after the show, the mouselings laughed when Lord Stilton's ghost wailed, "*More cheeeeeeese!*"

When he tripped on his robe, out tumbled Henry and Phoebe. "Oh ... ummm ... more cheese, anyone?" asked Henry.

Angelina's year:

When school is nearly over for the summer, Miss Lilly always puts on a new show. This June it was called "The Rose Flower Fairies". We practised hard, but it was worth it because everyone who came to see it just loved the show. Miss Lilly clapped louder than anyone, and that made us all feel really special.

Mrs Thimble sold jigsaw puzzles of the show in her shop. Which three jigsaw pieces will fit into the spaces to complete the picture?

Answer: Pieces 1, 3 and 5 complete the jigsaw.

Mum and Dad are the best
parents a mouseling could have!
When they came back from
a shopping trip, they had
a surprise present for me – and
it wasn't even my birthday!
I was SOOO excited!

What do you think Angelina hoped to find in the gift box?
Draw and colour a picture of something she would like.

TO Angelina

My best friend Alice and I helped out in the garden in August. I climbed a ladder and collected apples from the big tree and Alice mowed the grass. I ate lots of apples so I think I had the best job, don't you?

Angelina started counting the apples she collected, but stopped when she got to 10! Can you colour in 3 more rosy red apples below?

What do you do in August? Write about it here.

Two mice in a boat

One evening, Angelina was pretending to accept a trophy for winning the Chipping Cheddar Boat Carnival.

Her dad had won it four times when he was a mouseling, with his partner, Sammy Watts's dad. "I'm going to win it this year," said Angelina. "My boat's going to be a big white swan with a gold throne in it!"

At school the next day, Miss Chalk announced the plans for the carnival. "Alice will be working with Henry and Angelina will be decorating a boat with ... Sammy," she said.

Sammy was not very pleased at all.

Neither was Angelina. "Do I HAVE to do a boat with Sammy?" she asked.

"Yes," said Miss Chalk. "It's all about teamwork!"

Angelina and Sammy met up at the old boat house to talk about their ideas. But they couldn't agree.

"I'm not doing a sissy swan boat!" said Sammy.

"And I'm not doing a silly pirate ship!" said Angelina.

When Captain Millar came along to give them their boat, he could see they weren't getting on very well.

"What's your plan, mateys?" he asked.

"Swan princess boat!" said Angelina, nodding her head.

"No, pirate ship!" said Sammy firmly.

Captain Millar laughed.

"Well, you'd better decide soon!" he said.

Angelina nodded. "Yes, Sammy, we have to do what Miss Chalk said," she told her partner. "We've got to work as a team, side by side."

But they didn't. The first thing Angelina did was to paint a white line down the middle of the boat.

Angelina decorated one half and Sammy decorated the other!

"No going over the line!" said Angelina.

"I wouldn't go into your smelly swan half!" said Sammy.

"And I won't even TOUCH your pirate half," said Angelina.

Over the next few days, Sammy worked hard on his pirate boat. He made a Jolly Roger flag and a big cannon made from an old chimney pot.

Angelina borrowed a cardboard swan from the Theatre Royal and made a big gold and blue Swan-Princess throne, decorated with lots of frills and a crown on top.

But the boat was a mess!

"It won't float with that great big heavy cannon on it," said Angelina.

"What about that big bird's head?" said Sammy. "That's even heavier!"

Just then, along came Mr Ratchet, the builder. "I like your boat," he said. "What's her name?"

"She's called the Pirate King!" said Sammy.

"No, the Swan Princess!" cried Angelina.

They *still* couldn't agree!

On the day of the carnival Angelina and Sammy jumped into their boat, but it started to sink!

They threw things into the river to keep it afloat. But they had to get rid of so many things that all that was left was the flag!

"Oh, no! Look!" said Angelina. "We're floating away

from the bank. Where are the oars?"

"There," said Sammy, pointing to where they bobbed around in the water ...

"We've got to stop this boat!" said Angelina.

Sammy pointed to an old tree stump on the riverbank. "Grab one of those vines, Angelina!" he cried.

He held one end of the vine and Angelina held the other.

Then, "One, two, three!" said Sammy, and they threw it over the tree stump and pulled the boat to the bank.

Along came Mr Ratchet again. "What happened to the Pirate Princess?" he asked them.

Angelina and Sammy looked at each other. **The Pirate Princess!** Of course!

The other boats were all at Millar's Pond when Sammy and Angelina's boat arrived. But it didn't sail along the river – it arrived dangling from a hook on Mr Ratchet's old crane!

Angelina and Sammy's boat was decorated with things they had found on the riverbank. There was a cannon made from a log, and Angelina had made a pirate eyepatch from a leaf.

Captain Millar judged all the boats.

Henry and Alice's boat won first prize, but Captain Millar gave the special prize for the best teamwork to ... "Sammy and Angelina!"

"Well done, you two," said Mr Mouseling.

He pointed to his old partner, Sammy's dad. "WE never won the teamwork prize. We were always arguing about how to decorate our boat!"

Sammy and Angelina smiled at each other and both of them burst out laughing.

"You can keep the trophy, Sammy," said Angelina. "You deserve it."

Sammy shook his head. "No, you worked hard. You have it, Angelina ..."

Angelina's year:

september was the month I liked best of all this year because it was when the Fair came to town! We had such a good time! There were games and candy floss and ice cream to eat, and exciting rides and things like the Spooky House!

eeeeek!

arrrrrgh!

ooooooh!

Wooooo!

hoowwwl!

Where did Angelina take her little cousin, Henry?
Look at the pictures and tell the story in your own words.
Don't forget to make lots of spooky, scary noises!

Wooooo!

aaaah!

One day in October, we were playing in the woods. Alice raked up all the leaves that had fallen from the trees into neat piles. Well, I just couldn't help myself! It was TOO tempting! I kicked the leaves around and threw them up into the air like bits of confetti. Poor Alice had to start all over again, I helped though!

Angelina found a BIG acorn when she was out in the woods.
One of these pictures is different from the rest. Can you find
the odd one out?

Now, can you count the big orange leaves on these pages?
Colour in a leaf for each one you find, and write the number.

Henry's halloween

1 One day, Mr Mouseling was telling the story of the Chipping Cheddar Witch. "She chased the mouselings on her broom saying the magic words ..."

2 Angelina and Alice knew what came next. "Magic wand, do as I please," they said in spooky witch voices. "Turn these mice into stinky cheese!"

3 "What if she tries to turn ME into cheese?" said Henry. "Sprinkle pepper on her tail, and **she'll** turn into cheese," said Mr Mouseling.

4 "Don't be scared, it's only a story, Henry," said Angelina. "Come on, let's make our special costumes for the halloween party."

"You can be a ghost, Henry," said Angelina, putting a sheet over him. "NO, I want to be something scary to frighten the witch away," said Henry.

Angelina and Alice were busy with their tree monster outfit so Henry decided to make his own costume. "It'll be more scary than yours!" he said.

Outside, Mrs Hodgepodge was talking to someone in a black cloak and a pointy hat. "Ooh!"said Henry. "It's the Chipping Cheddar Witch!"

He rushed back inside. "I've seen the witch!" he said, but Angelina wouldn't listen. "I don't have time for your baby games, Henry," she said.

Angelina pointed to the door and Henry walked down to the kitchen. When he saw a little pepper pot he picked it up and ran into the garden.

Henry bumped into William. "Come on, William, we've got to catch the witch before she turns everyone into stinking cheese!" said Henry.

They didn't find the witch but they **did** see her giant shadow on the wall. "Oh, crumbs!" said William. "Follow that witch!" said Henry.

They followed the witch to Mrs Thimble's shop. She went inside and came out carrying a big pumpkin, then she walked off down the street.

William and Henry went inside. Henry bumped into a shelf and the lid fell off a jar of treacle. Treacle dripped all over his white ghost outfit.

William and Henry couldn't find Mrs Thimble, but they **did** see a big piece of stinky cheese on the counter. "It's Mrs Thimble!" they cried.

They ran outside and saw the witch in the distance. "This way, William," said Henry, pulling his friend along. "We've got to follow her. Come on!"

Angelina and Alice were in the forest where they had been collecting leaves for their tree-monster suit. When a tree creaked they stopped.

17

"What was that?" whispered Alice. "I hope it wasn't the Chipping Cheddar Witch," said Angelina. "Or a REAL tree monster ..." said Alice.

18

Henry was watching the witch from Angelina's garden when he tripped over a pumpkin lantern, spilling a cloud of pepper all over William. "Aaaa-chooo!"

19

Alice and Angelina were nearly home when Henry burst through the hedge. He was covered in leaves and twigs – and the pumpkin was on his head!

20

"Waaaaaargggh!" screamed Alice and Angelina. They ran away only to bump into – the witch! "WAAAAAARRGGGH!" they screamed even louder.

21 Henry sprinkled pepper on the witch's tail but nothing happened. That was because the "witch" was Miss Lilly in her halloween party outfit!

22 That night, Miss Lilly stood at the front of the ballet school stage. "It has been very difficult to choose the best costume this year, darlinks," she said.

23 "First prize goes to ... Henry, Alice and Angelina." The "tree monster" stepped forward, but tripped, and ended up on the floor in a big puff of pepper.

24 "Aachoo! Aaaachooo!" William sneezed, and his fang teeth shot across the floor. "Happy halloween, my darlinks," said Miss Lilly. "AaaaCHOOO!"

November was cold and rainy and everyone was feeling a bit fed up — especially me. Summer seemed a long time ago, and Christmas was weeks away. There was nothing to do and nowhere to go, until Dad came up with an idea. "We'll ask Grandma and Grandpa over, I'll play my fiddle and you can put on your best tutu and dance for us!" he said. Dad always comes up with good ideas, and that was one of his best. After that, November wasn't so bad, after all!

Look carefully. Which of the little pictures can you see in the big one? Write a tick ✓ or a cross ✗ in each box.

3   4   5   6

Answer: Pictures 1, 3, 4 and 6 are part of the big picture.

December is a l-o-o-o-n-g month. It's just not fair that we have to wait until almost the end of the month for Christmas Day to come! When I got home from school one cold and dark afternoon, Mum was busy making mince pies, but there was nothing for me to do. "I'll make up a puzzle for you," said Mum. "If you finish it before the mince pies are cooked, you can choose the biggest one!"

You can try Angelina's puzzle, too. Just find these names in the word square. They are spelled out from side to side and from top to bottom.

ALICE

DAD

GRANDMA

GRANDPA

HENRY

MISS LILLY
(2 separate words)

SAMMY

MUM

O	G	S	A	M	M	Y
G	R	A	N	D	P	A
X	A	L	I	C	E	L
M	N	U	V	S	K	I
U	D	A	D	Y	N	L
M	M	I	S	S	X	L
D	A	H	E	N	R	Y

Answer:

69

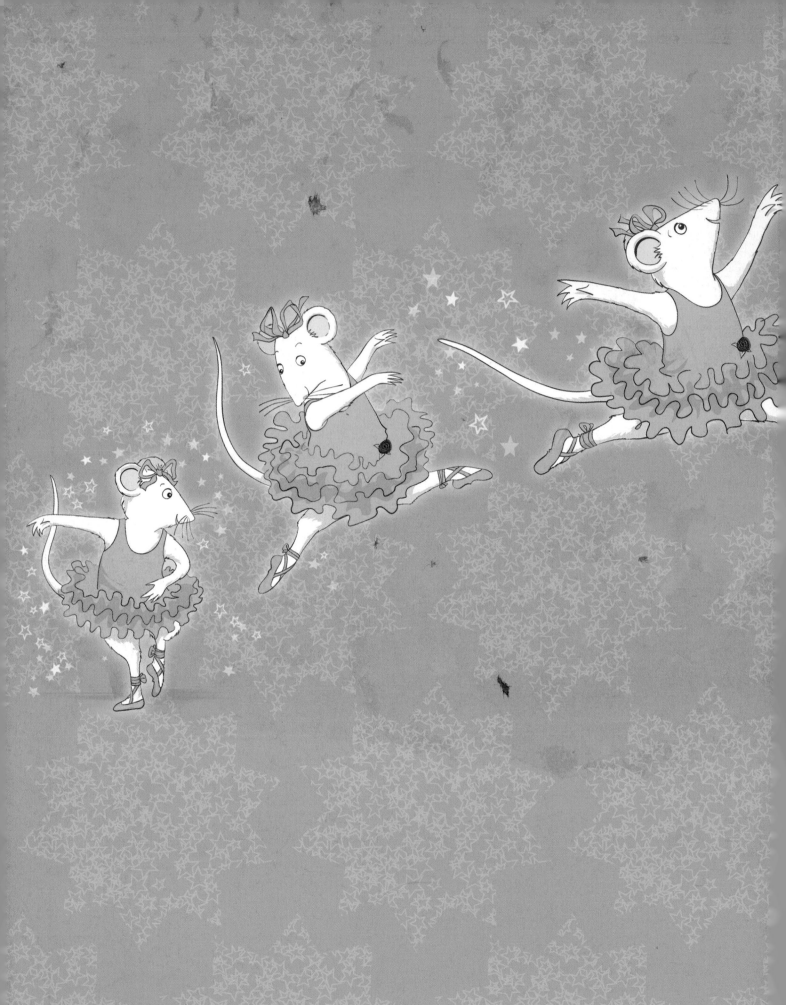